# Fight the Night

## TOMIE dePAOLA

**SIMON & SCHUSTER BOOKS FOR YOUNG READERS**

NEW YORK   LONDON   TORONTO   SYDNEY   NEW DELHI

*For Mia, Ian, Gene, Jack, and the Two Florences and Joes*

SIMON & SCHUSTER BOOKS FOR YOUNG READERS
An imprint of Simon & Schuster Children's Publishing Division
1230 Avenue of the Americas, New York, New York 10020
This book is a work of fiction. Any references to historical events, real people, or real places are used fictitiously.
Other names, characters, places, and events are products of the author's imagination, and any resemblance
to actual events or places or persons, living or dead, is entirely coincidental.
Copyright © 1968 by Tomie dePaola
Copyright renewed © 1996 by Tomie dePaola
Originally published in 1968 by J. B. Lippincott Company
All rights reserved, including the right of reproduction in whole or in part in any form.
SIMON & SCHUSTER BOOKS FOR YOUNG READERS is a trademark of Simon & Schuster, Inc.
For information about special discounts for bulk purchases, please contact Simon & Schuster Special Sales at 1-866-506-1949
or business@simonandschuster.com.
The Simon & Schuster Speakers Bureau can bring authors to your live event. For more information or to book an event,
contact the Simon & Schuster Speakers Bureau at 1-866-248-3049 or visit our website at www.simonspeakers.com.
Book design by Laurent Linn
The text for this book was set in ITC Highlander Std.
The illustrations for this book were rendered in black ink with pre-separated color overlays added in magenta and blue.
Manufactured in China
1119 SCP
First Simon & Schuster Books for Young Readers edition February 2020
2 4 6 8 10 9 7 5 3 1
Library of Congress Cataloging-in-Publication Data
Names: DePaola, Tomie, 1934– author, illustrator.
Title: Fight the night / Tomie dePaola.
Description: First edition. | New York : Simon & Schuster Books for Young Readers, [2020] | Summary: Deciding to fight the night
because it always comes at the wrong time, a boy spends an unusual night under the covers at the bottom of his bed.
Identifiers: LCCN 2019013285 | ISBN 9781534443730 (hardcover) | ISBN 9781534443747 (eBook)
Subjects: | CYAC: Night—Fiction. | Fantasy.
Classification: LCC PZ7.D439 Fi 2020 | DDC [Fic]—dc23 LC record available at https://lccn.loc.gov/2019013285

It was after supper and Ronald and his friends were
having a good time playing tag with Ronald's cat, Walter.

Then they played hide-and-seek.

Ronald was just about to come "in free" when Mama called,
"Time to go to bed, Ronald. Tell your friends good night."

"I don't want to go to bed yet," said Ronald. "We want to play some more!"

"But it's time for all of you to be in bed," said
Mama. "And besides, tomorrow is another day.
Maybe there will be a surprise for you."

"Even if I have to go to bed, I won't sleep,"
said Ronald. "I will stay up all Night!"

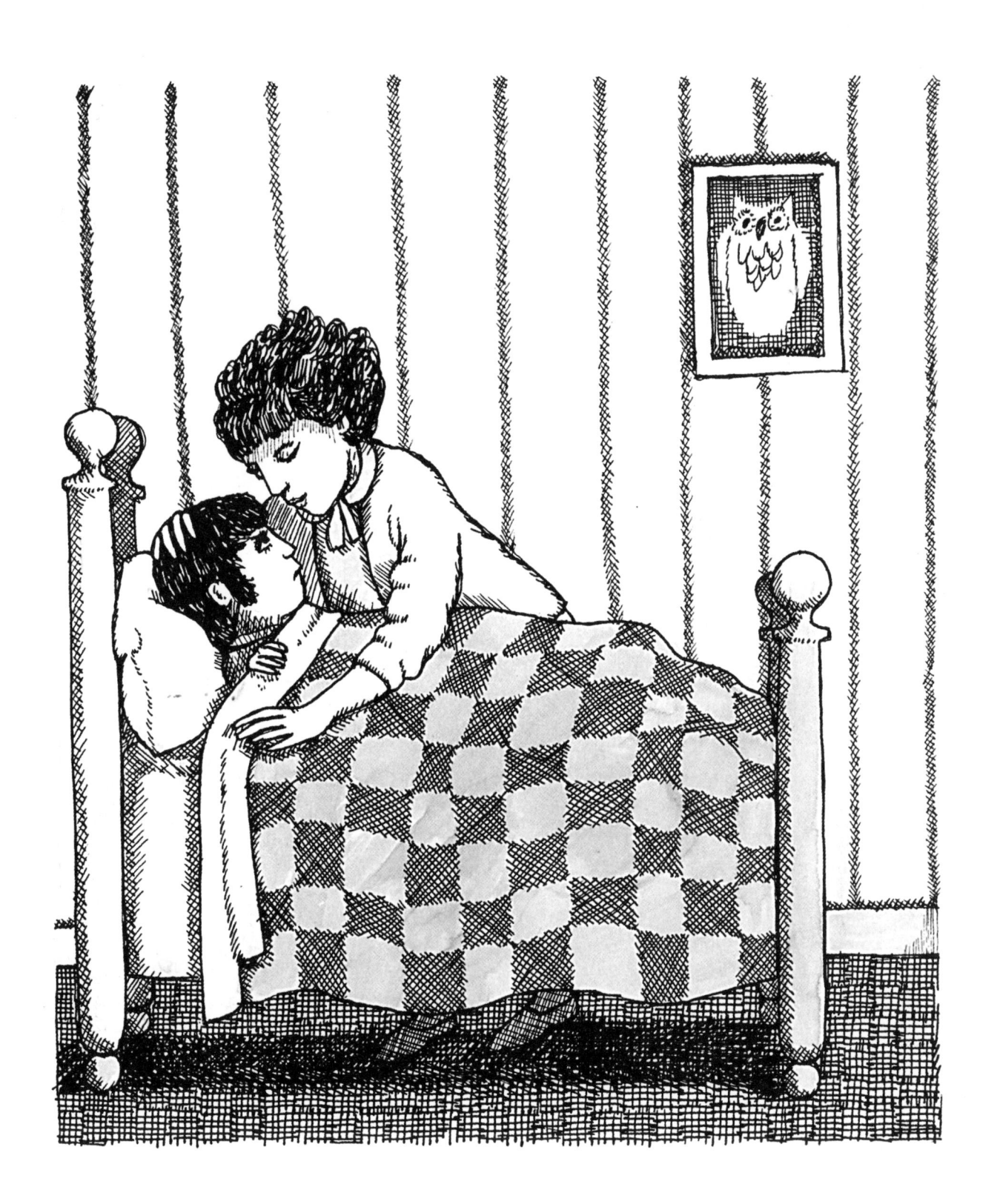

"All right," said Mama, "but when the Night comes, it will make you fall asleep."

"The Night is not my friend. It always comes at the wrong time.

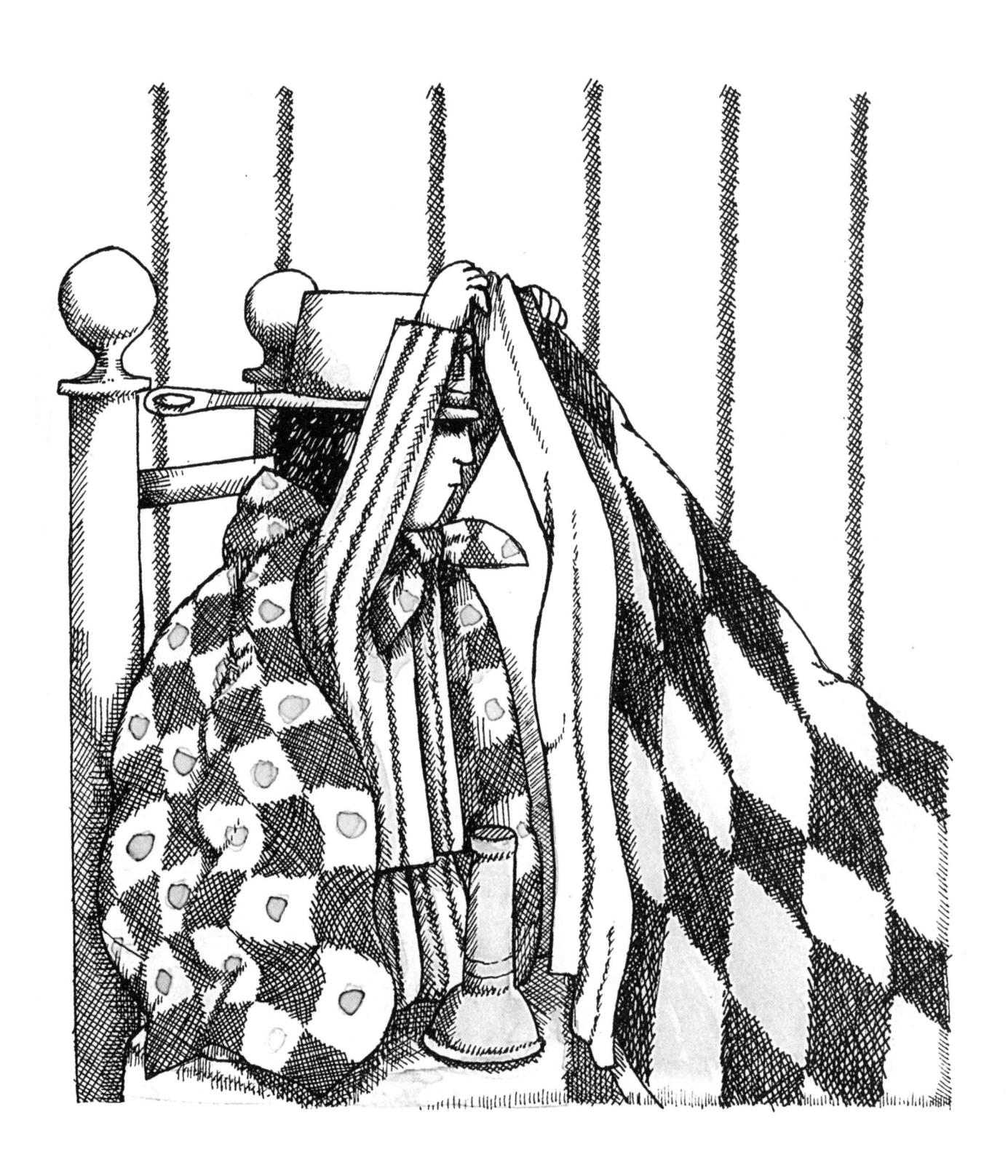

"I will Fight the Night," said Ronald, and he got his flashlight. He put on his helmet and cape and pulled the covers over his head, waiting for the Night to come.

It was dark under the covers, so Ronald turned on his flashlight. The bottom of his bed looked very far away.

"I will crawl to the bottom of my bed and wait for the Night there," he said.

When he finally got there, he squeezed way down,
and before he knew it, he was on the other side and it
was very dark.

As Ronald started to walk, he saw two eyes looking at him.

He shined his flashlight and there was Walter.

"What are you doing here, Ronald?" asked the cat.

"Where am I?" said Ronald.

"You are in the Nighttime," answered Walter.

"Good!" said Ronald. "I'm going to Fight the Night."

"You are silly," said the cat. "You'd better go home. I will not take care of you." And he ran silently and swiftly away.

Ronald heard a noise above him and he followed
the beam of his flashlight. There was an old owl.

"Why aren't you asleep?" said the owl.

"I'm going to Fight the Night," said Ronald. "Where is he?"

"You'll find out soon enough. And then you'll be sorry!" said the owl as he flew off.

Out of the darkness Ronald heard a voice: "Go to sleep before it's too late."

"No, I'm going to Fight the Night," answered Ronald. "Who are you?"

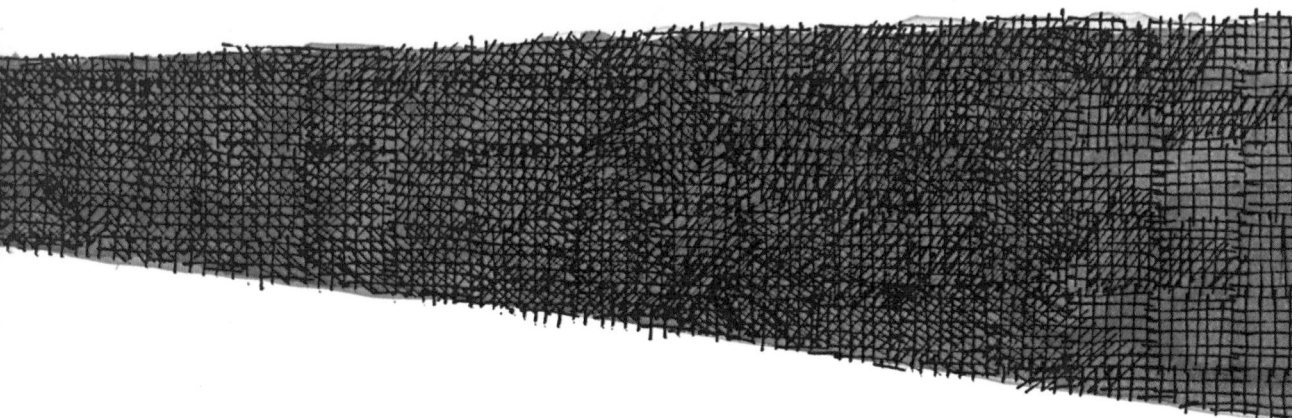

The voice whispered, "I'm the Night!"

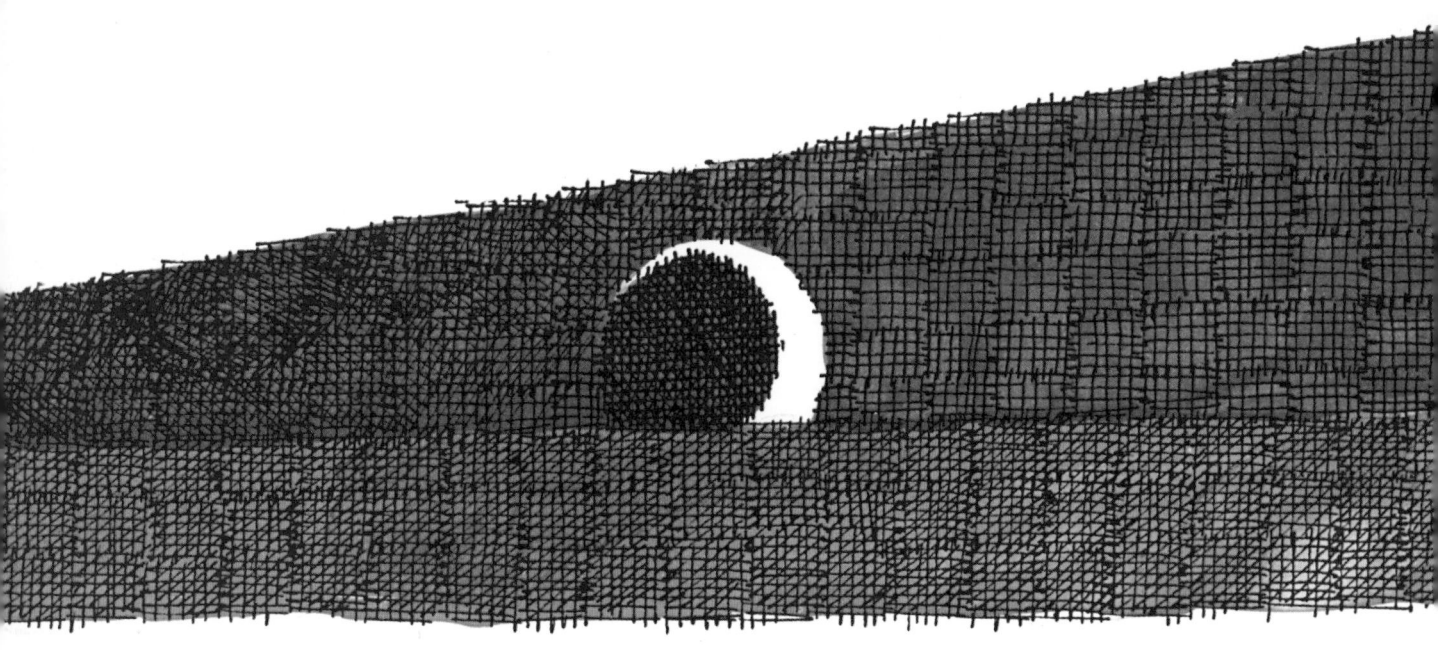

"Let's fight," said Ronald, and he began to swing his flashlight around.

"You will never catch me," said the Night.

Ronald heard a squeaking noise.
"I'll get you, Night," said Ronald, and he swung his flashlight.

"You missed," said the Night.

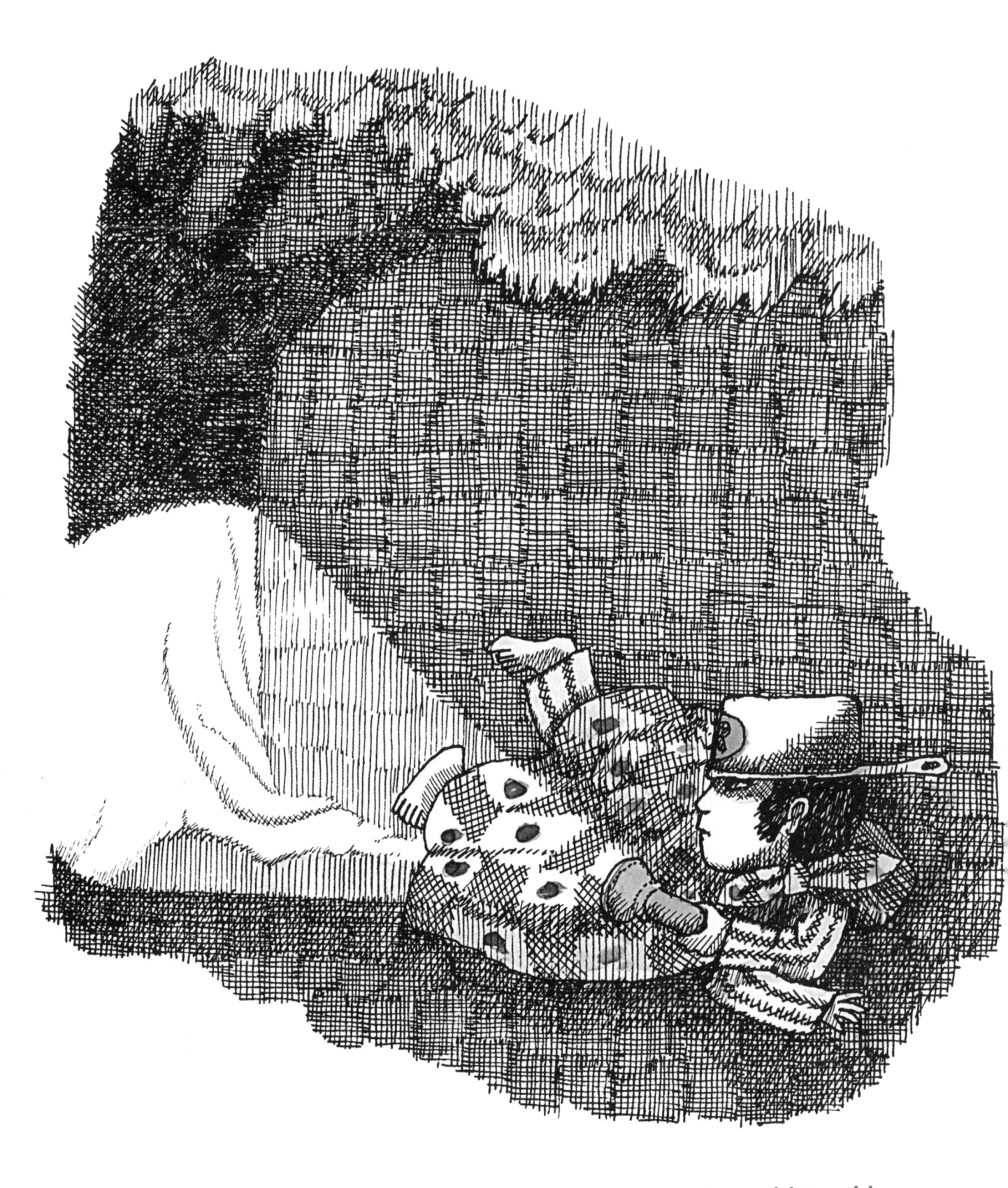

Ronald ran after the voice. Something tripped him. He swung his flashlight.

"That's not me. You cannot catch me. I am the Night."

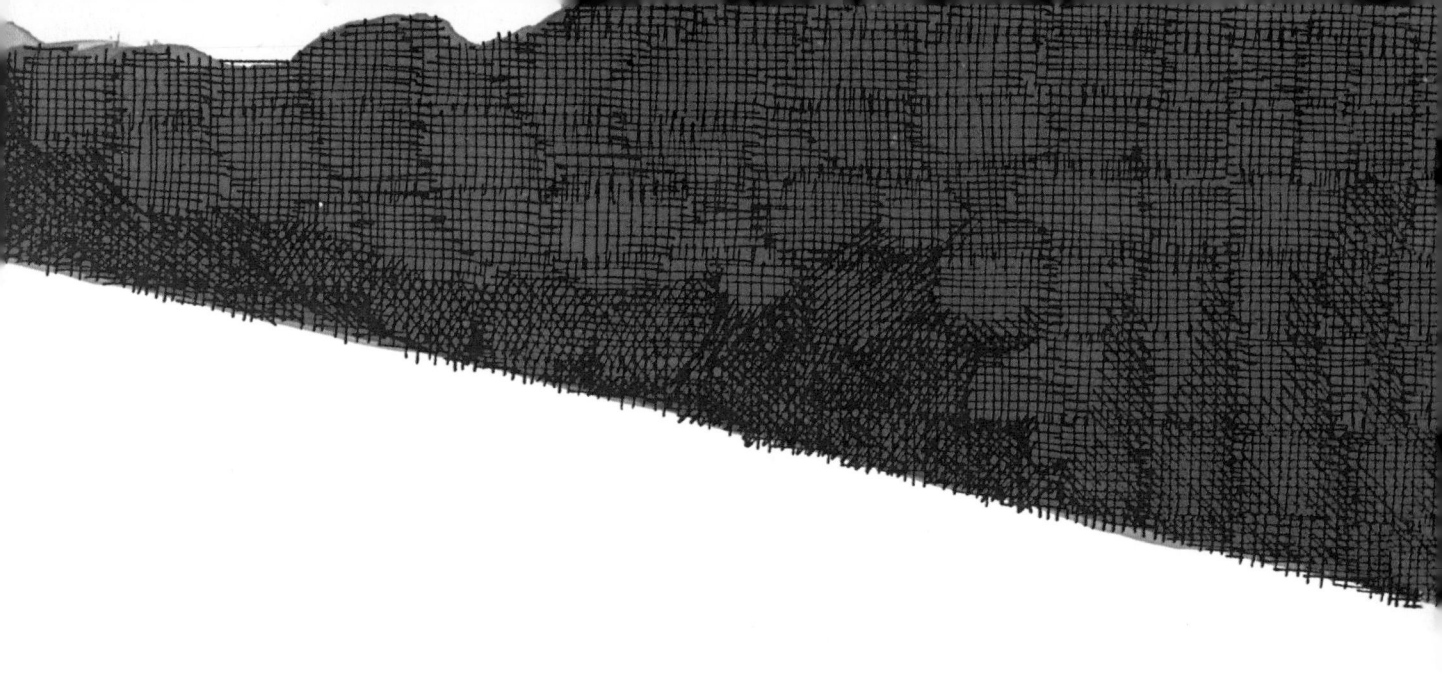

The voice came from everywhere all around. Ronald swung his flashlight right and left, but he found nothing.

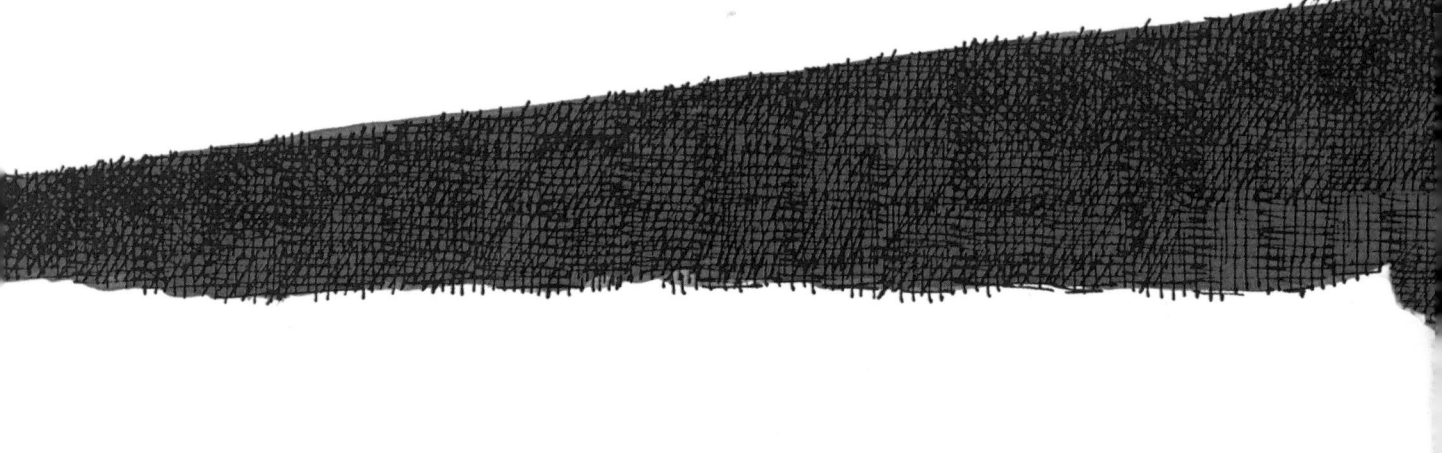

"Aren't you getting tired, Ronald?" said the Night.
"No!" said Ronald, but he was tired.
His arms ached and his legs ached.
"I must keep on Fighting the Night," Ronald said to himself, and he swung his flashlight, following the voice and Fighting the Night.

At last a rosy light started to shine at the bottom of the sky, and the Night was suddenly gone.

Ronald listened hard but no voice, no Night!

"I won. I won," said Ronald. "I chased the Night away." And he turned off his flashlight.

He crawled back through the end of his bed and crawled until he got to the top of his covers.

It was morning.

Ronald took off his helmet and cape and put away his flashlight. "Ronald, breakfast is ready," called Mama from the kitchen.

But Ronald didn't hear her. All he heard was the Night's
voice coming from under the covers at the bottom of the bed.
"Ha, ha, ha," whispered the Night. "I won, I won!"

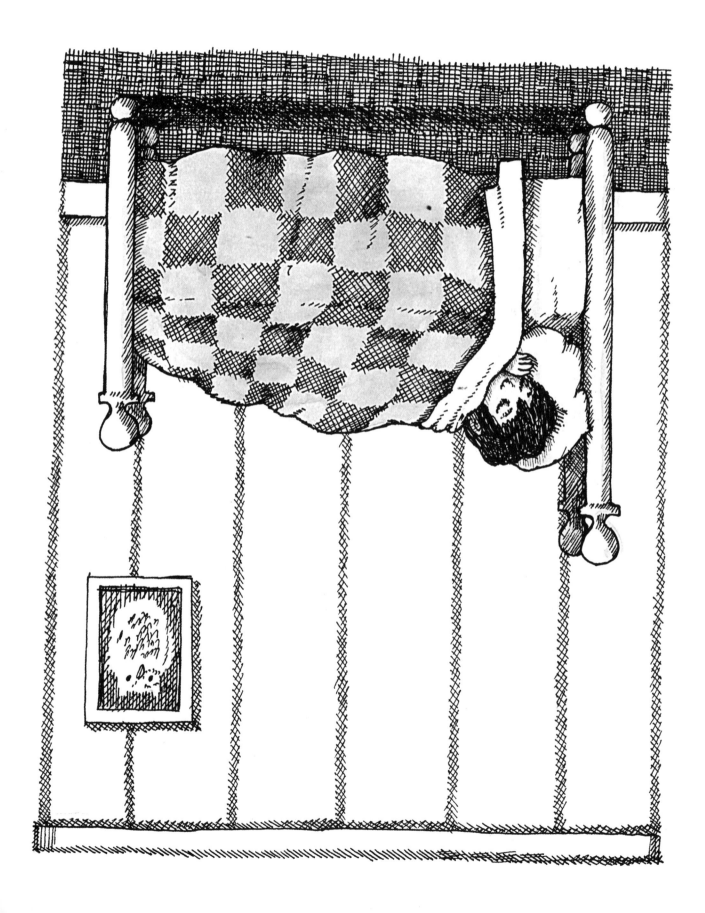

And Ronald slept all day.

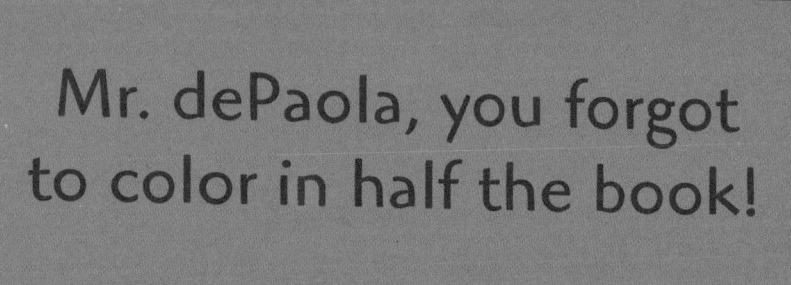

# Mr. dePaola, you forgot to color in half the book!

I've received many letters from kids saying this same thing about *Fight the Night*. And it's true that this book is only half in color. But I promise—I didn't forget to paint the black-and-white pages! As a matter of fact, I was only *allowed* to use color on every other page.

More than fifty years ago, when this book first came out, it cost a lot of money to print books with colored ink. To save money, the book publisher told me half the book had to be in black and white. Then, for the color pages, they would only let me pick two colors! I chose blue and magenta, which combine to make the purple you see in these pages.

Today, colored ink doesn't cost as much. I can use as many colors as I want—and on *every* page!